POKÉMON

TALES OF ADVENTURE

All rights reserved. Published by Scholastic Inc., *Publishers since 1920*.
SCHOLASTIC and associated logos are trademarks and/or registered
trademarks of Scholastic Inc.

The publisher does not have any control over and does not assume any
responsibility for author or third-party websites or their content.

No part of this work may be reproduced in whole or in part, stored in a
retrieval system, or transmitted in any form or by any means, electronic,
mechanical, photocopying, recording, or otherwise, without written
permission of the publisher. For information regarding permission, write
to Scholastic Inc., Attention: Permissions Department, 557 Broadway,
New York, NY 10012.

This book is a work of fiction. Names, characters, places, and incidents are
either the product of the author's imagination or are used fictitiously, and
any resemblance to actual persons, living or dead, business establishments,
events, or locales is entirely coincidental.

ISBN 978-1-338-18624-6

10 9 8 7 6 5 4 3   18 19 20 21 22

Printed in China   38

SCHOLASTIC INC.

POKÉMON™

THE RESCUE MISSION

"Look out, here I come!"
Bonnie shouted as she dove
into a big pile of leaves.
    Dedenne and Pikachu
laughed.
    They were all on their way
to the Pokémon Center in
Snowbelle City.

"Let's go, Bonnie," called her big brother, Clemont. He was a Pokémon Trainer. So were his friends, Ash and Serena.

Bonnie loved playing with their Pokémon. But she really wanted one of her own.

"So cute!" Bonnie shouted. A tiny green Pokémon had curled up inside her bag. It was sleeping. And it had the coolest pink mark on its tummy.

Bonnie knew she had to take care of it. She loved it already!

But when the little Pokémon saw her, it tried to hop away.

Bonnie grabbed it carefully. Then she showed it to her brother.

"Whoa!" said Clemont. "I've never seen that Pokémon before."

Ash checked his new Pokédex.

"Nothing," he said. "No data."

"So that means it's a new kind of Pokémon?" Clemont asked.

"Awesome!" cried Ash. "That's so cool!"

The little green Pokémon seemed scared.

"I'm going to take care of it," Bonnie decided.

"Bonnie!" Clemont warned. "You don't know anything about it."

But Bonnie knew she would learn.

"You're squishy," she told the Pokémon. "So I'm going to call you—Squishy!"

"*Pika pika*," Pikachu warned,
but it was too late.

The friends heard a loud
rumble.

The ground shook.

"Oh no!" cried Ash. "Dodrio!"

A herd of Dodrio ran by and knocked everyone over. Their friend Sawyer was trying to catch one with his Grovyle. Squishy got scared and bounced away. "Hey," Bonnie cried, "my Squishy's gone!"

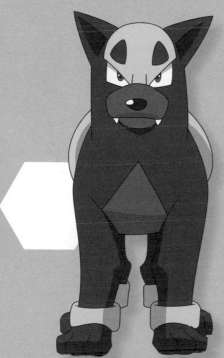

Squishy hopped as quickly as it could. But it did not get far.

Team Flare blocked its path. Their pack of angry Houndour growled.

"Trying to run away, are you now?" asked Team Flare's leader, Celosia. "We need you for Operation Z."

She called on her Drapion. "Pin Missile. Let's go!"

A large purple Pokémon with giant claws snatched Squishy.

Squishy squirmed, but it couldn't break free.

"Good," said Celosia. "Let's go back to the lab."

"You let Squishy go!" Bonnie shouted. She knew Squishy wanted their help.

"Please, what a bore," said Celosia. "Drapion, use Toxic."

Before Drapion could make a move, Ash stepped up.

"Okay, Pikachu," he said. "Thunderbolt! GO!"

"*Pi-ka-chuuuuu!*" Pikachu's cheeks sizzled with a bolt of electricity.

"Grovyle," Sawyer shouted. "Use Leaf Storm!"

Grovyle blasted Squishy out of Drapion's claws.

Ash quickly called on Noibat. "Use Supersonic!"

Drapion tried to fight back with Sludge Bomb. But Pikachu zapped it with one last Thunderbolt.

The Houndour shrank back. Team Flare ran away. Squishy was safe!

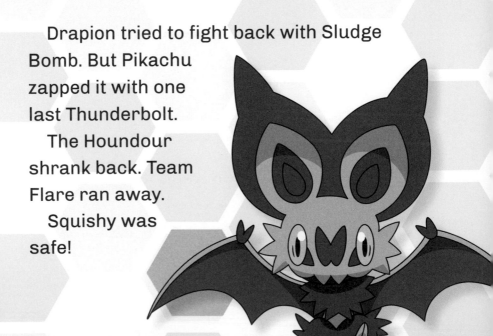

"Squishy, you're okay!" Bonnie scooped the Pokémon into a hug.

This time, Squishy did not try to hop away.

Ash, Clemont, Serena, and Sawyer threw their Poké Balls into the air. All their Pokémon came out to say hello.

Squishy bounced up and down happily.

Soon all the Pokémon were sitting in a circle sharing food and water.

Pikachu held out some fruit. But Squishy would not eat it.

"*De ne*?" Dedenne tried to share a berry.

Squishy shook its head.

Bonnie was worried. They'd had such a big day!

"Squishy, aren't you hungry?" she asked.

Squishy jumped up as if to say, "Don't worry. I don't need food."

It bounced over to a rock and curled up in a tiny patch of sunlight.

The pink mark on Squishy's tummy began to glow.

Squishy fell asleep smiling.

Bonnie's brother was confused, but Bonnie had an idea.

"Maybe all it needs is sunlight," she said.

"Wow!" said Serena.

Bonnie felt proud. They were learning about Squishy just by taking care of it.

The friends crawled into their tents and fell asleep. But Squishy woke up in the middle of the night with a bad feeling.

Team Flare was back. Squishy knew it. This time, the Pokémon was not scared.

Squishy hopped into the forest. It would protect its new friends. And its new friends would protect Squishy.

"Squishy, wait up!" Bonnie cried. She ran after her Pokémon.

"*Pika pika!*" Pikachu called.

"I told you that Pokémon is mine, see?" Celosia held out a Poké Ball.

"Well, you're wrong," declared Ash. "If Squishy was yours, you wouldn't treat it the way you do!"

"Enough!" Celosia barked. "Dark Pulse!"

Her pack of Houndour shot sonic waves at Bonnie and her friends.

"Frogadier, Water Pulse," Ash shouted. "Pikachu, Thunderbolt!"

While Ash and Sawyer fought, Clemont, Bonnie, and Serena grabbed their Pokémon and ran for safety.

Bonnie held Squishy close.

But as they crossed a river, Bonnie slipped on a rock.

Squishy fell into the water.

It was carried downstream far away from Bonnie—right to Team Flare's Bisharp!

"We've got you now," said Celosia. "You're a Core Zygarde, and we need you for our experiment. So give it up."

Houndour and Sneasel snarled.

Squishy took a big hop backward.

Squishy wanted to find Bonnie and stay with her.

But it would need help.

If it really was a Core Pokémon like Team Flare said, then it must be the center of something big.

Squishy closed its eye and sent out a call.
A mass of glowing Pokémon Cells came
together around Squishy.
They spun and twirled until suddenly,
Squishy took on a powerful new Forme!

Squishy's new Forme roared, and rays of light burst up from the ground.

"Retreat!" Team Flare screamed. They started running away.

From down the river, Bonnie heard the roar.

"It's Squishy, I know it!" she cried. She raced toward the sound.

"Squishy!" Bonnie ran to her Pokémon and hugged it tight.

"I won't let you go again," she said.

Squishy cuddled close. Bonnie had taken good care of the little green Pokémon, and it wasn't going anywhere without her.

POKÉMON™

TEAM ROCKET TO THE RESCUE!

"Best friends forever . . ." Bonnie sang to her Pokémon. "We're so happy together."

"Wow, Bonnie, what a nice song," Ash said.

"*Pika, Pika!*" Pikachu agreed.

"I call it the Squishy song!" Bonnie told her friends.

Bonnie had found Squishy— the Core Zygarde—on the way to Snowbelle City. She was on a journey with her brother, Clemont, and their friends Ash, Pikachu, and Serena.

Bonnie kissed her new Pokémon on the head. They were already best friends.

"I promise I'll never leave Squishy," she sang. "My sweet Squishy, that's you!"

Bonnie did not know that Team Rocket was watching her. They wanted to steal Squishy! As the Core Zygarde, it had amazing powers.

Jessie and James called their boss to tell him about the rare Pokémon.

"I've never seen a Pokémon like it!" James said.

"Then catch it before anyone else does," the boss said. "I'm counting on you."

"He LOVES us!" Meowth sang. Team
Rocket was so happy, they felt like singing.
   "And a searching we will go!" Jessie said.
   "We're outta here, yo!" Meowth howled.
They blasted off to catch Squishy.

Back by the river, Squishy was trying to nap. But something was wrong.

"Hey, Squishy," Bonnie said. "Pancham and Chespin wanna play."

Squishy was not in the mood to play. It sensed that its friend Z2 was in trouble. But Squishy was too tired to move.

"I think you're sad," Bonnie said. She tried to sing her Pokémon to sleep. She knew Squishy got its energy from the sun.

"I'll care for you and always be with you," she sang.

Squishy closed its eyes. The little Pokémon felt safe. It hoped that Z2 would be safe, too.

But Z2 was not safe. Team Flare's Weavile was chasing it through a cavern.

Druddigon blocked its path.

Z2 was trapped!

"Excellent work," said Aliana, a member of Team Flare.

Team Flare was even more dangerous than Team Rocket. They wanted to catch Z2 for their boss, too. And they had a plan.

"Z2, you're coming with us," said Mable, another Team Flare member.

But Z2 would not go without a fight.

Z2 jumped high over Druddigon's head.
"Weavile, let's go!" Mable shouted.
Weavile pounced on Z2, but Z2 blasted it with
a green force field.
Before Weavile could attack, Z2 sent out a call
for help. Other Zygarde Core
cells came from all over
the canyon. They joined
together to form a
powerful Zygarde.

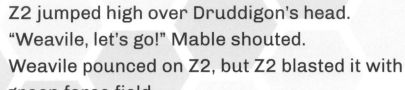

Zygarde let out a roar and charged at Druddigon's belly.

Druddigon slammed back against a cliff.

"Do it!" shouted Mable.

Team Flare aimed their blasters at Zygarde. But Zygarde was too fast. It ducked and weaved between the blasts.

"Use Dragon Pulse!" Aliana yelled.
Druddigon built up a powerful ball of
energy and aimed it at Zygarde.

Rocks shattered around the Legendary
Pokémon.

"Use Metal Claw!" Mable shouted.
Weavile swiped its sharp claws at Zygarde.

Zygarde twisted its body and swatted Weavile away.

With a mighty roar, Zygarde let loose a giant ball of energy.

The explosion sent Team Flare flying. Zygarde ran for safety.

As it ran, the Zygarde Core cells scattered. Zygarde turned back into Z2.

Z2 bounced right into the clutches of Team Rocket!

"Squishy?" Jessie asked.

"No, its markings are different," James said. "Perhaps there's more than one Squishy."

"What luck!" Jessie cried. "We've struck Squishy gold!"

"You're ours now!" Meowth purred.

But Team Flare stood in front of Team Rocket with their blasters aimed at Z2.

"It's the glasses gang!" Team Rocket shouted.

Jessie threw herself on top of Z2 to protect it. James and Meowth piled on top.

They would not let Team Flare steal their boss's new Pokémon!

"Inkay, destroy that ray!" James called. "Psybeam, touché."

Inkay's Psybeam knocked the blaster out of Mable's hand.

"All right, Gourgeist," Jessie called. "Use Seed Bomb!"

Team Flare fell to the ground in a storm of seeds.

Team Rocket fled with Z2.

"Ugh, I can't run anymore," Jessie said.

They ducked behind a large rock.

"Let's take a cab next time," said Meowth.

Z2 whimpered in James's arms.

Jessie remembered
spying on Squishy and
Bonnie. "That twerp's
Squishy gets its energy
from the sun," she said.

"Time for some tanning," James said. He
scampered up a tall rock and placed Z2 on top.

Z2 soaked up the sun's rays.

"Success!" James said. "You're green with
health."

"You're not getting away this time," Aliana
called.

Team Flare was back. "Playing tag is
pointless and boring."

"Not on your life," James said. He cradled Z2
close to his chest.

"Dragon Pulse, go!" Aliana called.

Aliana's Druddigon blasted Team Rocket.

But James's Wobbuffet used Mirror Coat to send the pulse right back at Druddigon.

The giant Dragon-type Pokémon fell with a grunt.

"Wobbuffet rules!" Team Rocket shouted.

But the battle was not over yet.

"Use Icy Wind!" Mable called to her Weavile.

Weavile flew high into the air and blew its frozen breath right at Team Rocket. The cold gust sent them blasting off again.

"Now let's wrap this up," Aliana said.

Team Flare's Pokémon circled Z2.

But Z2 still had some moves of its own.

It sent out a call for help. Zygarde Core cells came from all over the cliffs and beyond.

Z2 grew into a bigger, more powerful Forme of Zygarde.

"That power," Aliana said. "It's the real deal!"

Zygarde roared. It unleashed a Dragon Pulse so strong it blasted a crater into the ground.

Team Flare hid behind a rock.

Zygarde reared up, ready to let loose another giant pulse.

"Oh no!" Aliana said. "Not again."

"*Char!*" A Charizard swooshed in and scorched Zygarde with Flamethrower.

A stranger stepped up beside Mable and Aliana. "The boss sent me to buy you some time," he told Team Flare. "Be ready."

"Now Charizard," he called. "Use Dragon Claw!"

Zygarde was too strong for Charizard. With one swat, it blasted the Fire-and-Flying-type Pokémon.

The stranger spoke into his wristband. "Respond to my heart, Key Stone!" he said. "Beyond Evolution! Mega Evolve!"

Team Flare watched as Charizard became Mega Charizard X!

"Dragon Claw!" the stranger called.

Mega Charizard X swooped into the air and attacked Zygarde with a fiery rage.

Dodge. Hit. Slam.

Mega Charizard X and Zygarde rammed into each other with equal force.

"Full power, now!" Mable ordered.

Team Flare blasted Zygarde with everything they had.

The force was too much for Zygarde. The Zygarde Core cells fled. And Zygarde turned back into Z2.

"End of the line, Z2," Mable said.

She grabbed the Pokémon and placed it into a glowing cage.

Back in the woods,
Bonnie scooped up
Squishy into a big hug.
She could tell when
Squishy was sad.

"Everything will be
okay," she told Squishy.
"I'm right here with you."

Squishy and Bonnie would find Z2 and
rescue it from Team Flare.
But for now, Squishy was happy to have a
best friend like Bonnie to keep it safe.

Ash, Cilan, and Iris were taking a break outside Castelia City. While Cilan made lunch, Ash and Iris decided to give Scraggy and Axew a little practice.

"*Scraggy!*" the little Dark- and Fighting-type cried.

"*Axew, ax!*" Axew cheered.

The practice battle began.

"Okay, Axew, Dragon Rage, let's go!" Iris said.

But Axew couldn't control the attack. Dragon Rage blew up into the sky like fireworks.

"Well, we tried!" Iris laughed.

"Hey, gang! Lunch is all ready!"
Cilan called.

As he lifted the cover from the
food, a Ducklett swooped in and
stole the silver top!

"Ha, ha, ha!" the Ducklett laughed
as it ran off.

Then something even stranger happened! The ground beneath Ash and Pikachu started to move. Suddenly, the Trainer and his best pal were falling through a long, dark tunnel.

"*Whoooooa!*" Ash yelled as he slid down, down, down.

Ash and Pikachu landed at the
bottom of a mountain. A Sandile
wearing sunglasses greeted them.
But it wasn't just any Sandile. . . .
   "Hey, aren't you the Sandile we
battled back at the Hot Sands Spa?"
Ash asked.

"*Sandile, sand,*" it said, nodding. Sandile had brought Ash and Pikachu to the bottom of the mountain for a rematch!

"What do you say, Pikachu?" Ash asked his Pokémon.

"*Pika, pika!*" Pikachu cheered.

Just then, a Ducklett wandered onto the middle of the field.

"We're kind of in the middle of a battle. Would you mind moving to the sidelines?" Ash asked.

Ducklett refused to move. So Sandile nudged it with its nose.

Ducklett tickled Sandile's nose with the feathers on its wings.

"*Achoooooo!*" Sandile sneezed so hard, its sunglasses flew off its face. Ducklett grabbed the sunglasses and put them on.

"*Sand, sandile.*" Sandile asked for its favorite pair of shades back. Ducklett took them off. But instead of handing them back, Ducklett blasted Sandile with Water Gun!

"Ha, ha, ha!" Ducklett laughed. It flew away with Sandile's sunglasses.

Sandile was sad. It really loved those sunglasses.

"Don't worry, Sandile! I'll get your glasses back!" Ash promised.

"*Pika!*" Pikachu agreed.

"*Sandile, sand,*" Sandile thanked them. It was happy to have friends to help.

Just then, another Ducklett
swooped in. It snatched Ash's hat.
"Hey, give that back!" Ash yelled.
Ducklett didn't like being shouted
at. It shot Ice Beam at Ash.
Ash dodged Ducklett's attack. But
the Water- and Flying-type still flew
off with his cap.

Ash, Pikachu, and Sandile chased after Ducklett. It led them to a riverbank, where it joined the Ducklett that had stolen Cilan's cover and the Ducklett that had stolen Sandile's sunglasses.

"Now we've got to deal with three of them!" Ash cried.

Ash was fed up. He was ready
to battle. But three Ducklett
versus Pikachu and Sandile
wasn't a fair fight.

"Ha, ha, ha!" the Ducklett
laughed at them.

"Pikachu, use Thunderbolt!" Ash cried.

"*Pikaaaachuuuuu!*" Pikachu yelled, zapping the Ducklett.

But one of the Ducklett was able to dodge the attack. It flew right into Pikachu and Sandile with Wing Attack.

One Ducklett splashed Ash with Scald. Then another trapped Ash in Ice Beam.

"Man, that's cold!" Ash shivered from inside a big block of ice.

Sandile bit through the giant ice cube and freed Ash.

"Hey, Sandile . . . thanks!" Ash said.

Meanwhile, the Ducklett had flown into a tree house. Ash, Pikachu, and Sandile ran after them.

The Ducklett threw stuff at them—
a soccer ball, a broken chair, a red
guitar, a pink umbrella. Pikachu tried
to unleash Thunderbolt, but it got
trapped inside the umbrella.

"*Pikkkaaaaaaaaa!*" Pikachu
yelped. It was caught in its own
Electric-type attack!

Ash and Sandile risked getting zapped to pull Pikachu out of the pink umbrella.

"Pikachu, are you okay?" Ash asked.

"*Piiiiikaaa,*" it sighed as it shed extra electricity.

Suddenly, the Ducklett swooped back in, shooting Scald.

"Come on, let's get out of here!" Ash yelled to Sandile.

"Ha, ha, ha!" the Ducklett laughed.

Ash and his friends hid and spied on the Ducklett. "Man, look at all the stuff they've got," Ash sighed.

Ash, Pikachu, and Sandile were outnumbered. So Ash came up with a new plan. He walked right up to the Ducklett.

"We don't want to fight you. We just want our stuff back," Ash explained.

It seemed like the Ducklett were moved by Ash's speech.

One Ducklett slowly walked over to Ash, Pikachu, and Sandile. It held out the sunglasses.

"Wow! You're going to give them back?" Ash said.

But when it got close, Ducklett surprised them with Water Gun.

"Ha, ha, ha!" the Ducklett all laughed.

There was only one thing to do: stand up to these bullies!

"Pikachu, use Thunderbolt now!" Ash yelled.

But Pikachu's Electric-type attacks weren't working right. So Sandile stepped in.

"*Sandile!*" it said. It wasn't afraid of Ducklett anymore. Now it was all fired up!

"We're here if you need us, okay?" said Ash.

It was three against one! Plus, Ducklett's Water-type attacks were very powerful against a Ground-type like Sandile.

But Sandile had smarts on its side. It started with Stone Edge, a Rock-type move that was very effective against Ducklett.

One Ducklett fired back with Ice
Beam. Another Ducklett shot Scald.
And the third one used Water Gun.
"Dodge them, Sandile!" Ash cried.

Sandile was in trouble. The three Ducklett were overpowering it. So Pikachu stepped in with Iron Tail to help block the attacks.

But the Ducklett trio zoomed at them. They knocked Ash, Sandile, and Pikachu around with Wing Attack.

Suddenly, Pikachu blasted the Ducklett away with an incredible Electro Ball.

"Whoa, Pikachu!" Ash said. He was amazed by his Pokémon's powerful new move.

Pikachu's Electro Ball was so bright that Cilan, Iris, and Axew were finally able to find their friends in the forest. Ash quickly told them everything that had happened with the Ducklett. "You mean there are actually three Ducklett?" Cilan asked.

Just then, the three Ducklett swooped back in. They spurted Scald at the three friends.

"What's wrong with you guys?" Iris cried.

"Such behavior is hard to understand," Cilan said.

Ash and Pikachu had had it. "Pikachu! Use Thunderbolt!" Ash cried.

"*Pikachuuuu!*" yelped Pikachu, firing the attack.

That scared the Ducklett off for good!

"Way to go, Pikachu!" Ash cheered.

Sandile thanked Ash and Pikachu for their help. "*Sandile, sand.*"

"Well, those Ducklett caused a lot of trouble, but because of them, Pikachu learned a brand-new move! Right, buddy?" said Ash.

"*Pika, pika!*" Pikachu agreed. It was ready for its next adventure in Unova.

POKÉMON™

BLACK & WHITE

EMOLGA MAKES MISCHIEF

It was a bright and sunny day. Ash, Cilan, Iris, and their new friend Bianca were walking through the woods. They were on their way to Nimbasa City.

"Way to go catching Emolga, Iris!" Ash said. Iris had just captured the wild Electric- and Flying-type.

"Let's have a battle between Emolga and my Pignite," said Bianca.

"Okay! I accept your challenge," said Iris. She took Emolga out.

"It's so cute!" Bianca squealed.

"Emolga, use Hidden Power," said Iris.

Pignite fired up Heat Crash.
Emolga countered with Attract.
Instantly, Pignite was surrounded by
hearts. Emolga had charmed it!
"Pigniiiiiite," it sighed. It stared
at Emolga with hearts in its eyes.

"Pignite, return!" cried Bianca.

"Good battle strategy, Iris!" cheered Cilan.

"My next Pokémon is Minccino," said Bianca. She told Minccino to use Tickle.

"*Emo emo,*" Emolga giggled.

"Quick, Emolga, use Hidden Power!" Iris shouted.

Emolga let out a burst of light. But it also snuck in a Volt Switch. Emolga disappeared from the battle and another of Iris's Pokémon took its place!

"*Excadrill!*" cried Iris's Ground- and Steel-type. It landed with a thud.

"Huh?" Iris said. Emolga had used Volt Switch to escape the battle. It had put Excadrill in its place!

Emolga giggled at its trick. Bianca and Iris had to laugh, too.

"Emolga, what's the point of having this battle if you're going to use Volt Switch?" Iris asked. "Since we're doing this for practice, I hope you'll do what I ask you to."

Emolga burst into tears.

"Now you made Emolga cry!" exclaimed Ash.

"Emolga! Please stop crying," Iris pleaded.

Iris was worried about Emolga. It just didn't seem to want to battle.

"Building trust between Trainer and Pokémon is what training is all about," Cilan said.

"You have to be friends first," Ash agreed.

"A Pokémon battle can be fun if you put your heart into it, Emolga!" Iris told her Pokémon. "What do you say we give this rematch with Pignite one more try?"

Emolga shrugged. It didn't seem to care about Iris or the battle.

But Iris was determined to continue. She told Emolga to use Hidden Power. The little Pokémon obeyed. Then it used Volt Switch to disappear again!

"Emolga, where did you go?" Iris worried.

Iris searched the woods for Emolga. She found it sleeping in a tree.

"Emolga, come down here this instant!" Iris yelled.

But Emolga ignored her. So Ash's Snivy stepped in and used Vine Whip to carry it down.

"Why don't we take a food break?"
Cilan suggested.

Cilan handed a piece of fruit to
each Pokémon. But one piece wasn't
enough for Emolga. It used Attract
to get Tepig, Oshawott, Swadloon,
and Scraggy to hand over their
lunches.

When Emolga's spell wore off, the other Pokémon didn't know what had happened to their food. And they were very hungry! The four Pokémon started to fight.

"*Pikachuuuu!*" Pikachu yelped. It broke up the scuffle with a mighty Thunderbolt.

"Hey, what's going on here?" Ash asked.

"I think they're mad because someone stole their food," Cilan said.

"Who would do that?" asked Iris.

Snivy pointed to Emolga. Ash's Pokémon had seen the whole thing, and it wasn't fooled a bit.

"Just a minute!" cried Iris. "Emolga wouldn't do an awful thing like that. Would you, Emolga?"

"*Emo emo!*" Emolga cried. Tears rolled down its face.

"See?" said Iris.

"Guess you're right. Sorry!" said Ash.

Lunch was over, and the Trainers were ready to go. Until...

"I feel a little sleepy!" Ash said, yawning.

While the four Trainers took a nap under a big tree, Emolga woke up and sneaked into the woods. Oshawott and Axew decided to follow it.

Emolga was still hungry. It found a tree full of fruit in the forest. But a pack of wild Watchog was in the tree, and they didn't want to share.

Just then, Axew and Oshawott came down the path. Emolga decided to trick them. It told them that the Watchog had stolen the fruit from it.

"*Osha!*" Ash's Water-type Pokémon was angry. So Oshawott used its scalchop to slice some fruit off the tree for Emolga.

The three Watchog didn't like that one bit. They came after Oshawott. But they missed and slammed into a big tree. Ouch!

The loud noise woke a wild Simisear. It stormed over and fired a fierce Flamethrower. The Watchog were terrified. They ran away.

Oshawott tried to defend its friends. But Simisear knocked it against a tree. Axew didn't know what to do.

As for Emolga, it bit into a fruit like it had nothing to do with all this trouble.

The giant Simisear stomped up to Emolga. The little Pokémon finished its fruit and threw the core right at Simisear's nose.

"*Emo emo!*" Emolga laughed.

That made Simisear really angry. The big red Pokémon took a couple of swings at Emolga. But the fast Electric- and Flying-type dodged the Fire-type's fists.

"*Emo emo!*" cried Emolga, laughing again.

Now Simisear was boiling mad! It wound up a big punch to hit Emolga and Axew.

That's when Snivy came to the rescue! It had secretly followed Axew and Oshawott into the woods. It stopped Simisear with Vine Whip.

"*Simiseaaaaaaaar!*" the wild Pokémon shouted, firing Flamethrower.

Emolga tried to run away from the fight. But Snivy used Vine Whip to drag it back. This time, Emolga had to clean up its own mess!

Simisear shot another fiery
Flamethrower. Snivy protected its
friends with Leaf Blade. But it could
not avoid Simisear's Fire Punch. *Pow!*
   "*Snivy!*" the little Grass-type cried
in pain.

Just then, Iris, Ash, Bianca, and Cilan found the Pokémon in trouble.
"There they are!" cried Ash.
"Quick, Emolga!" Iris called.
"Help everyone out!"

Emolga looked around. The other
Pokémon were in big trouble! And
it was all Emolga's fault. The little
Pokémon realized it had to do
something.

So Emolga bravely jumped into the
battle. It flew around Simisear and
blasted it with Hidden Power.

Simisear tried to fire back with Flamethrower, but super fast Snivy tripped it with Vine Whip.

Simisear's Flamethrower shot into the cliffs above and broke off a huge rock. The boulder was headed right for Simisear's head!

"Simisear!" it cried out for help.

Emolga and Snivy were ready!
Emolga used Hidden Power to break
up the rock. Then Snivy used Leaf
Storm to blow the fragments away.

"Snivy, you were great!" Ash said.
"You, too, Emolga!" cheered Iris.
"Sim simisear," said the big
Pokémon, thanking them.

Iris was bursting with pride for her Pokémon.

Emolga smiled. It was proud of itself too. It picked up the last fruit on the ground and handed it to its new friends, Axew and Snivy.

"*Emo emolga,*" it said, thanking Snivy for its help.

Snivy cut the fruit into three pieces so they could all enjoy the snack.

"It appears those three are now friends!" Cilan declared.

Emolga smiled. From now on, it would be there for its buddies.